The Stag and The Mother Moon

D.O. Scissom

Published by D.O. Scissom, 2024.

This is a work of fiction. Similarities to real people, places, or events are entirely coincidental.

THE STAG AND THE MOTHER MOON

First edition. March 8, 2024.

Copyright © 2024 D.O. Scissom.

ISBN: 979-8224853021

Written by D.O. Scissom.

To my own Mercer Kinfolk, for filling my life with magic and grace. For empowering and emboldening me every day. Thank you, I love you all.

The Red Mountain Pentecost Revival

"**B**rad, where are we supposed to turn again? I thought it was only six miles off the main road, but it feels like we have been driving through these woods forever."

Diane poked her brother in the arm, she knew he wasn't sleeping, but he was ignoring her and pretending to. She should have driven the first leg, and let him drive them in. She hated driving on these narrow mountain roads. Their dad's Ford station wagon barely fit as it was, and in the fading light, she was having a tough time seeing the edges of the road.

Brad finally stirred, "Stop poking me, just stay on this road until you see the signs, it's county road fourteen, and the white cross on the left, is Red Mountain Pentecost Revival. Then turn left there and it's another mile down the road, but it's supposed to be the only thing at the end of the road." He closed his eyes and laid his head back again.

"I don't know why we have to do this anyway, why aren't Mom and Dad here if this is so important? We don't know any of these people, but we are spending a weekend here for some party or something."

Brad turned to face his younger sister. "Diane, I don't know what else to tell you. Mom and Dad got a visit from some old guy, then the next morning said we had to drive down here to

Alabama for this church deal, some family thing, but it had to be the two of us, and we had to come right now. It was the same conversation you heard. I don't know what else you want me to say, that this is some fat city? Because I don't like a second of it, but our parents are great, Mom and Dad take care of us and if going to this moldy church out in the boonies means this much to them, then we are there. I am not even sure what you are mad about, you didn't have anything better to do, I totally had a date with Ella this weekend, and I did not want to miss it if you know what I mean."

Diane rolled her eyes at this; she hated it when Brad talked like that about Ella. She and Ella had been best friends for two years, and now that she was dating Brad, she barely had time to hang out, plus she hated the way, he insinuated Ella was easy. Ella was a good girl, and so pretty. She honestly did not know what Ella saw in Brad, she was so out of his league, but he was a year older than them and had his own car, and a part-time job at Miller's grocery. But still, she just couldn't see it. With her long black hair and dark brown eyes, her cheerleader's figure. She was just the picture of the perfect woman, and Brad was just Brad.

He was right though; she had no plans, and her mom had made this sound important. It had something to do with the church where she grew up, her mom was from Alabama, right outside of Birmingham, on Red Mountain. This was some kind of family reunion, and church event combined. Some selection, or vote, they were vague about the details. They just said there would be a bunch of cousins and relatives there, and that she and Brad would have to be there as well. She asked if there was a vote or something and what her mom wanted her to do, and she just said everything would be explained to them and to pack for three days and leave immediately because it was about an eight-hour drive.

Take two days of casual clothes, and her Sunday best for church and dinner on Sunday, they would drive back after that. They were sending them with gas money and a cooler with food, everything else would be provided for them while they were there. Dad would give Brad a little extra for a hotel on Sunday night if things went late, but not to use it unless they just could not safely make it home on Sunday.

It all seemed so strange, their parents never talked about their life growing up in Alabama, and the kids had never met anyone else in their families. Not aunts, uncles, or grandparents. No cousins or anything, anytime anyone asked about it their parents just said there was no one there worth meeting. None of it made sense to her but she knew that either way, there was no getting out of it. She thought about appealing to her dad most of the time, a little whining and she could get her way with him.

But it was clear, even to her, that this wasn't a time to even attempt it. Dad barely spoke during the whole conversation, a rare thing indeed, and more than that, Mom was in charge, like completely in charge and that was probably the thing that threw her off the most. Mom was never in charge, not really, she always let Dad do the talking and always let him make decisions. No matter how hard she thought about it, she could not remember any time that Dad had just sat by while Mom did all the talking. He just appeared sad and defeated and it made her scared. Her mom, however, mom seemed somehow larger and more present than she had ever seen her. Like she had been hiding herself for Diane's entire life and now suddenly, she was showing who she was, awakening somehow.

"Diane, dammit Diane, now we have to back up you missed the turn!"

Brad was yelling from the passenger seat.

Sure enough, she had been daydreaming, and she missed the turn.

Diane wheeled the big car into the driveway at the end of the small dirt lane. There was a modest house at the front of the property, and the drive wrapped around behind it. As they rounded the corner of the property they almost ran over a huge man in a poorly fitting suit. The jacket barely fit his broad shoulders and barrel chest.

"Help you folks?"

Brad sat up straight, "Evening sir, we are Brad and Diane Whistler, I think we are supposed to be meeting some family at the church here."

"Patricia's kids? Wonders never cease, I guess that makes me your Uncle John. John Wilcothe. But we can get into that later. Head on around the bend, and you will see the lights as soon as you get around the barn, park along the line of the other cars there, careful though, the ground is still soft, and you don't want to get your car stuck. The rest of the family is already in the chapel, just go on in. Revered William and Judith are in the foyer greeting newcomers until the meeting starts, they'll get you situated."

At that, the man turned and lumbered off toward the house.

As they entered the chapel Brad and Diane were met with the sound of an out-of-tune piano being played with far more enthusiasm than talent. Diane played piano, and there was something about the way these keys were being hammered that just didn't sound right to her. Not that the pianist didn't know how to play, but that they were playing under duress; like they were angry at the keys or something else and were taking it out on the keys.

A voice as raucous as the piano interrupted her thought.

"Oh, children come in, come in, introduce yourselves, and let me get a look at you."

The man was red in the face and sweating, Diane thought to herself he looked like the kind of man who was always sweating. His black hair was thinning, and combed over his balding scalp in an attempt to hide the fact that he would soon lose it all. The woman at his side was the picture of a country preacher's wife. Dressed in an ankle-length brown dress and flat shoes, her chestnut hair was piled high in a bun so tight as to appear painful. Diane noticed her lack of makeup and jewelry immediately. She made a mental note to ask her mother if that was part of the church rules or something.

Brad stepped forward with his hand outstretched, "Brad Whistler sir, pleased to meet you, and this is my sister Diane."

He turned and Diane stepped forward and offered her hand as well. Diane heard the woman next to the Reverend suck in a sharp breath.

"Very nice to meet you, Miss." The Reverend did not offer his hand. He continued in that overbearing, made-for-the-Sunday-pulpit voice. "This is my lovely wife, Judith."

Diane was only sixteen, and while she may not have been sure of much in her young life. But she was damn sure that this man was the only person who had ever referred to his wife as lovely. Cunning, determined, strong, more than she seems, but never lovely. She was broad-shouldered with a square face and broad forehead. Her hands looked more designed for wringing the necks of chickens and slaughtering hogs, than nurturing children or offering comfort to the distressed.

You forgot dangerous, she's very, very dangerous. Diane did not know whose voice it was in her head, but it was clear as day. She looked around confused for a moment before the voice continued. *The woman you're looking at is far more dangerous than you can know, be wary and be guarded.*

Before she could react or even process the woman wrapped a strong hand around her upper arm and pulled her away from the men. "Come then, let the men talk important business, and let's see if we can find you something that fits. You cannot enter our lord's house dressed as you are and the hour is growing late, everyone is waiting. While I am not surprised Patricia's children are late, I am shocked she did not warn you that you would not be allowed into our chapel dressed like a whore."

Diane tried to pull away from that iron grip, and Brad said, "Hey you can't talk to her like that, I don't care who you are."

Judith scowled and Reverend Wilcothe put a hand on Brad's shoulder to calm him down.

"Now Mother." The Reverend scolded "Diane here did not grow up in our traditions through no fault of her own. Her willful mother, my youngest sister, in case you were wondering,"

He nodded at Brad at this as if to say, you know little sisters, then continued. "She took you all away from the family church as soon as she married that Whistler fellow, everyone else of course, tried blaming him, as if anyone could convince your mother to do a thing, she did not want to do herself. I have the scars to prove otherwise, I tell you, and so do more than one of the church and family elders. Meaner than a rattlesnake, your mother. You will meet more than one person this weekend who would not say a cross word to your mother if she was planted in front of them, even now." At this, he stared at his wife, his look was making it clear how he felt about her comment.

Judith lowered her head and voice. "It makes no difference what she knows or does not know, or why, she cannot enter the chapel in short sleeves and a skirt so short I can see her knees and wearing makeup. I have a skirt I can pin up; and a sweater to cover her arms until she can be fitted for some proper clothes for Sunday Service."

Diane started to protest, she did not care a lick about what this woman thought, or her wacky traditions, if the good Lord took issue with seeing a woman's arms or shins, he should have made them uglier, like this woman. Again, that voice, familiar, spoke straight into her mind, no, deeper than that. Like it was speaking to her soul. *Not now, do not anger this woman any more than is absolutely necessary. It will be tough enough to keep you safe without her deciding you are an enemy.* Diane listened and followed Judith down a side corridor.

Down the hall, they passed a series of doors, each one marked with a different bible verse on the door. Diane knew a couple of them, John 3:16, Mathew 5:10, Luke 6:23, odd she thought about the meaning of those verses together, God's love and sacrifice, combined with a persecution complex. No wonder these people were messed up. God gave his only begotten son, and everyone hates you, and you are better off for it. The door at the end was also marked, 1 Timothy 2:9-15, she couldn't remember what this one was and stood staring a moment.

Judith snorted derisively, "In like manner also, that women adorn themselves in modest apparel, with shamefacedness and sobriety; not with braided hair, or gold, or pearls, or costly array but which becometh women professing godliness with good works. Let the women learn in silence with all subjection. But I suffer not a woman to teach, nor to usurp authority over the man, but to be in silence. For Adam was first formed, then Eve. And Adam was not deceived, but the woman being deceived was in the transgression. Notwithstanding she shall be saved in childbearing. If they continue in faith and charity and holiness with sobriety. "

Diane stared at her for a moment. She wanted to throttle the woman, wanted to slap her face; and watch the blood pour from her judgmental mouth. She was surprised at herself. Her entire life, she had never talked back to her parents, she had never been disrespectful to a teacher or authority figure of any kind.

But this woman, in just the space of a few minutes had driven her to rage, made her completely forget herself and actually long for violence. She pictured herself with a club or sword cutting this woman down like some knight of old, and she was repulsed with her imagination and lack of propriety.

Judith continued. "A couple of your cousins also showed up dressed, immodestly." She snarled the last word, and Diane was dying to mock her by screaming "like whores," but she controlled herself.

That voice again. *If you want to make it through this unscathed you must control your thoughts and words. If she sees you as a threat she will react, and you cannot imagine how cruel she can be.*

Diane felt like she was going crazy, drove eight hours to the middle of nowhere to land in Crazy Town, and now she had to change clothes to make some wacko happy because the voice in her head was telling her to. This could not be real. Judith opened the door and motioned ahead.

She heard panicked voices and scrambling, "We are changing."

"Shut the door please."

Judith barked, "I am aware of what you are doing, I am the one who forced you all to have some decency and modesty. If only any of your parents had taught you to cover yourselves as our Lord and Savior commands, we could have skipped this little exercise."

Diane entered the room quickly hoping Judith would shut the door behind her just as quickly, to spare the women inside as much discomfort as possible. Judith of course did not shut the door but just held it open while she spoke.

"There are skirts and sweaters on the hangers in the corner, and some pins and sewing supplies are in the box on the desk. Please be quick, skirt must be below the knee, arms must be covered. Take off all your jewelry and wash off your makeup then back down the hallway and join us in the chapel as quickly as you can. We only have a couple of people left to arrive and Reverend Wilcothe would like to get started so we can be done with this business."

As she spoke Diane looked around. There were three other women in the room in various stages of undress. A brunette, petite and slender, wearing a girdle and a slip, was turned away from them, holding a shirt up to her chest and glancing back over her shoulder glaring at Diane and Judith. On the opposite side of the desk stood two of the most interesting women Diane had ever laid eyes on. They looked like identical twins as far as she could tell, she had never met twins before. Both of them were tall, over six foot, and as pale as Greek statues, with snow-white hair.

The one on the right wore high-waisted, pink lace underwear and a matching bra. The girl on the left was completely naked, she made no effort to hide her body but stared boldly at the newcomers. Diane tried to avert her eyes and found that she could not. She took in the sight of the bold woman, every inch of her skin appeared as flawless and white as a porcelain doll.

Again, she tried to look away but instead looked directly at the woman's face, making eye contact. *My goodness, I could fall into those black eyes,* she thought to herself. *If I don't look away now, I may never look away, I may die of old age, staring into her eyes.*

Judith broke the silence, "Insolent, immodest, harlot, have some decency and cover yourself. What if the reverend or one of the other men had been with me?"

The woman smiled darkly and stared right at Diane when she spoke, "Then they would have looked at me with the same hungry look as your little friend there. Or maybe the rumors about the men of this church are true and I have aged out of their interest."

Judith lunged forward, "Spew that filth in my presence again and I'll drag you to the yard as you are and switch you for the world to see. "

At this, the other twin dropped the shirt she was fussing with and stepped in between the two women. "Aunt Judith, if you lay a finger on her, or me, or any other woman here, not only will I come for you, but you know what will follow. The entire Lewis clan will descend on this place, and The Choosing will be the least of your worries. You know who, and what, we are. My sister and I are here to fulfill our obligation to our mother's family so that no harm befalls the innocent. But if you presume to hold any power over us again. I may call down a hell that rivals any your poisoned mind can imagine. Remove yourself from us, we will change clothes and abide the traditions but remember what I said. Just because you cannot be chosen and you bore no children of your own, does not mean that this meeting is without peril for you. Now be gone and let us change in peace."

Judith spun and stomped out the door, slamming it behind her.

Diane looked between the three women again, she felt on the verge of panic. Her chest was tight, and her vision blurred at the edges. She grasped the chair in front of her to try and steady herself. "I don't understand what's going on, can someone explain to me why I am here." She could not control her emotions anymore and her voice shook, and tears began streaming down her face. "I just don't understand." She was ashamed of the fear and uncertainty in her voice.

The brunette rushed to her and swept her up in a hug, motioning to the other women, "Oh hey sweetie, I bet you don't. Come on, let's get you changed so we can get you some answers."

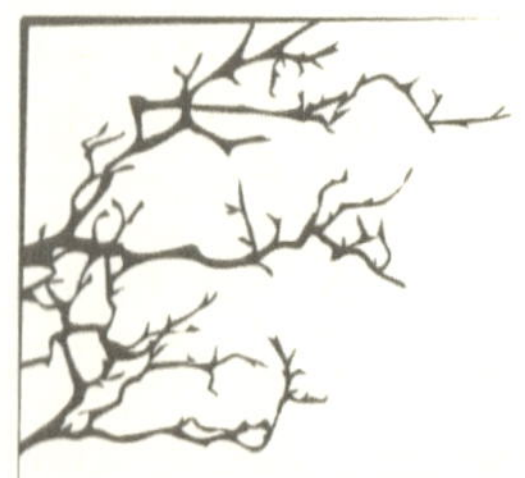

The Kiss

Diane was guided into the chapel by the three women she had changed with, Jackie, the brunette, and the Lewis twins, Desma, and Althea. Although once they were dressed, she could not tell them apart. They offered her little in the way of explanation, saying only that it was better for her to hear the whole story at once.

They comforted her through her near hysteria and gave her some advice. Jackie rubbed her shoulders and spoke softly, "When we get inside the chapel, all of us kids sit up in the first few rows, men on the right, women on the left. Do not try and sit with your brother, the more you disturb the setup and push back during this part the longer it will take to get your answers and start worrying about the things that matter. So just try to relax and realize nothing bad is going to happen tonight but there is going to be a lot that will be extremely difficult to believe. You can spend your time saying, this can't be real, this can't be real, or you can get to the important stuff and make the best of the time you have."

As foreboding as that all sounded, Diane was oddly comforted. The day had been strange enough, like landing in Oz, and all that had happened was some out-of-the-ordinary behavior on the part of her parents, a long boring drive, and meeting some super religious aunt and uncle, out in the middle of nowhere.

She desperately wanted to see Brad though, he would surely understand this a little better, and she needed his blind optimism right now. They walked into the chapel together two by two, Jackie walking in front with Desma, and Diane alongside Althea. She laughed to herself at the thought of the four of them walking each other down the aisle, like they were all marrying each other.

What a gas, she thought to herself, wouldn't these old country women flip their wigs at the thought of two women just throwing the idea of needing a man out, and marrying each other? *Sure, I'll wear a dress, and Althea can get a tux, she's so much taller than me, she would look great in a tux.*

She grinned like a buffoon at the thought. She would have to remember to tell Brad this when they got back to the car, he would howl.

She looked up and down the rows of pews for him, there he was, two rows back from the front on the right-hand side, next to the aisle, he was leaning forward, arms on the back of the pew in front of him and his head bowed as if in prayer. That was strange, it wasn't like he was exceptionally pious, perhaps slightly more than her, but this seemed out of character, maybe he was just resting from the long day. She desperately wanted to talk to him, and leaned that way as they passed, but Althea squeezed her arm and pulled her back on track. Diane looked at her to protest and the taller woman mouthed "Not now," and kept them moving to the front row on the left side.

Once they were seated, she was fully two rows in front of Brad and could not see him without turning around whatever was going on, she did not want to make it any worse and Desma sure seemed to give her the impression that's what would happen if she did. The piano kept banging along, a sturdy-built redhead in a plain grey dress hammering out a slightly out-of-tune and off-tempo hymn of some sort. Another bad rendition later and Diane was starting to get a little impatient, she wanted to check on Brad, she wanted to know what was going on. Most of all she wanted this craziness to end so they could high tail it out of here.

There had to be twenty-five or more young people and another twenty other adults, maybe more. The man from the end of the driveway walked to the front of the chapel, knelt at the small bench, and began to pray. A moment later Reverend Wilcothe stood up from his place at the front row of pews on the side opposite hers. He was red in the face and sweating profusely, he knelt next to the man and began praying with him. Althea looked at her and mouthed "Brothers."

Diane mouthed back, "Uncles".

She turned just in time to see Judith staring at her with open contempt. She wondered what she did to the woman to make her hate her so much, and more than that she wondered what the woman would do to her if she got the chance. She seemed angry just for anger's sake, and this whole thing was getting stranger by the minute. After a few moments, the reverend stepped onto the platform and got behind the pulpit, his brother joined him, sitting on a small but ornate wooden bench, behind and to the right of the reverend.

The reverend bowed his head and spoke. "Kinfolk, we are gathered here in this holy house, in our father's precious name. Will you bow your heads and pray with me, precious Jesus, we come to you seeking peace and blessings in these darkest of times Lord. You know what is in our hearts Lord, and your will be done, for yours is the kingdom and the power and the glory, in your most holy name, Amen."

The call of "amen" was loud from the back few rows, a sparse few were heard from the younger people closer to the front. Diane looked around again as the Reverend Wilcothe began speaking. "I wish that it were happier times that brought us all together family, would that we were gathered for a celebration, a wedding, a birth, even a homegoing."

"Blessed Jesus, blessed Jesus." Someone called from the back.

Wilcothe seemed not to mind. "Instead, we are joined here, in this chapel as we have for time out of mind to fulfill an obligation, to uphold our end of an unholy bargain. I would love nothing more than to spin you a yarn about how this was passed down from on high, about some noble calling that our family and many other families must fulfill to keep our lord's covenant on earth. But, alas, that is not the case. I cannot even tell you with honest truth about exactly how it started. Only what I know and what I have witnessed with my own eyes. You see children, it is our duty and our cross to bear, that once a generation a monster, a haint, a devil, walks among us and he chooses for himself and his unholy bride, four. That's right kinfolk, four of God's precious children to take unto himself for his own purposes. He and his devilish mistress, his whore of Babylon, they steal from our families, four of our youth for their own, and for what and what becomes of them, we cannot know."

The Reverend pulled the microphone from its holder on the pulpit and began to pace behind his brother, still kneeling in prayer. "What we know, what cannot be disputed is that the devil walks our beautiful mountain, that the good Lord has allowed our faith in him to be tested, like his faithful servant Job. In that test, he asks of us, complete obedience. I know that for those of you raised away from our church and our mountain this will all be hard to believe but I promise you it is very real. Tonight, and tomorrow, we will fellowship and prepare, and on Sunday, a demon and his hell bride will walk the very aisle of this sacred chapel, and they will draw from your number, four, that will accompany them back to whatever pit they come from. I promise you children, this has been the case for every generation as far back as anyone in the history of our great family can remember. We are not the only afflicted ones. The Milburn, Lewis, and the Holsapple families, and many more. It is our burden to carry and carry it we must, or."

"Or I will slaughter this entire bloodline and all who are attached to it." The deep voice boomed across the chapel like was amplified. At first Diane did not see where it was coming from.

Behind John Wilcothe, the air began to haze and blur, the big man started to rise, and a hand shot forward out of the haze and wrapped around his right shoulder, it was enormous, long black nails, that looked as sharp as an eagle's talons, dug into the man's shoulder through his suit jacket. He bowed his head again and whimpered a prayer. Then began to rise off of the ground as the arm lifted him. He grit his teeth against the pain but could not hide it. Gasps went up from the people gathered in the pews.

A woman in the back started to cry out. "Keep me, O Lord, from the hands of the wicked; preserve me from the violent man; who have purposed to overthrow my goings."

The haze cleared behind the preacher's brother and what stood there was the largest man Diane had ever imagined. *Not a man, an angel.* the voice in her head whispered. *If you can recognize him for what he is, a true angel, you may make it through this trial. You are about to witness something amazing.*

Standing just to the side of the pulpit, he had to be eight feet tall, not counting the crown of antlers that sprouted from the top of his head. Easily four feet across and another foot tall. The giant shook the man hard, and blood splattered from the wound where his nails dug into the flesh. He was naked except for a fur or animal skin that wrapped loosely around his waist, his bare chest was broader than the pulpit and covered in dark hair, damp with sweat. The ease with which he shook the big man around and held him one-handed off of the ground told Diane all she needed to know about his strength. Why did the voice call him an angel? she thought to herself.

People screamed, and still the woman prayed. "Oh God, the Lord, the strength of my salvation, thou hast covered my head in the day of battle."

The giant spoke again, his voice resonant like a radio broadcaster. "My love, would you ask her to stop making that noise so we can be about our business."

Diane heard a gagging sound and more gasps and crying, and she and Althea spun around at the same time. A woman, almost as tall as the giant on the pulpit, stood near the rear of the church, and had picked up one of the women from the pews. She held the woman aloft by her throat with her left hand, two fingers of her right hand were in the woman's mouth and appeared to be fishing around for a grip on her tongue.

She wore a loose silk wrap that rode high on her thighs and was open from the collar to her navel in a wide V, from what Diane could see she was completely covered in tattoos, everywhere except her face. Upon her head, a glowing crown of three moons, the waxing crescent moon, a full moon, and a waning crescent. When she spoke, Diane could feel the sound in her bones more than hear it, and the building seemed to shake with the power of words.

"If she would stop squirming, I would lay her foul tongue on the offering plate and bring it to you myself, my sweet prince."

Her words shook Diane's bones. What kind of witchcraft was this? *The oldest and most powerful in all the world, and your birthright Diane. Do not be afraid.* The voice in her head was comforting. But this was terrifying.

"I believe she now sees the error of her ways my dear, and I hope everyone else does as well. Also Reverend, I cannot tell you how much I do not like the name demon or devil, it's simplistic and reductive and implies that I am either a minion of your false god or reside in a fictitious hell. I can assure you, neither is true. Let me ask you Reverend, do you love your wife?"

The Reverend nodded his head slowly.

"I love mine as well, and have loved her for thousands of years, one thing I can promise you, that is true, if you cast one more aspersion on my bride, or use one more derogatory name in reference to her, I will skin your wife alive, and make my love a dress from it. Then I will burn everyone you have ever loved as an offering to her on your behalf."

He turned to face the gathered congregation and raised his voice even more.

"Does everyone understand what I am saying, if any member of this family says a disparaging word about my bride, I will kill all of you, you will watch one another tortured to death? All because of this man's inflated sense of self-righteousness and faith in a false deity. Reverend, I understand how your faith works, I understand that in your limited way, you truly believe that there is an all-knowing, all-loving God sitting in heaven somewhere that cares about your fate. I can promise you that is not the case."

He gestured around in a circle as if indicating every direction around him.

"See, there is a God, a creator, so to speak. But you are looking in the wrong place. Do not cast your eyes to an unseen power in a place that does not exist. Rather look at the evidence around you. Do not thank God for this beautiful mountain where your family has lived for generations, but acknowledge God in the mountain. I see you, God, in all your creations, I see you in the mountain, I see you in the river, I see you in the dog and cat and most of all I see you in me and my fellow men. Can you imagine it Reverend, looking in the mirror and acknowledging the divine energy in yourself? Oh, how you would see the world, imagine too, looking at the people who share the world with you and acknowledging the divine energy in them. Can you treat yourself and everyone else you encounter like the manifestation of God that they are?"

The reverend sucked in his breath, steadying himself, his voice shaking, but his fear did not stop him. "They exchanged the truth about God for a lie and worshiped and served created things rather than the Creator, who is forever praised, Amen. Because of this, God gave them over to shameful lusts."

The giant's voice echoed through the chapel even without amplification. "Do not quote that trash at me. I was there when the book of Romans was written, I knew the hand that penned it and the political motivation behind it. I promise you; no God had a hand in that, and I will not be lectured to from a collection of hate mail from one group of ignorant shepherds to another."

Diane looked upon the giant, the monster, or whatever he was. Still holding the reverend's brother by the shoulder, the man dangling at his side like a bag of groceries. But now that she could see him, not the shock of his appearance or the threats of violence. But really see him. His curly brown hair, and smooth face, his eyes so dark they might be black. She thought of the Lewis twins next to her, and their eyes, so similar. There was something so sincere, so authentic, about the way he smiled and spoke. He was terrifying to behold, and the things he said, the promises of violence. Still, Diane felt an honesty in his words, and his passion when he spoke of the creation, and of his bride, that made her believe him.

As much as she felt wrong for even thinking it. Of the three men on the stage in front of them. The giant, half-man, half-stag, who appeared out of nowhere, and had threatened to kill them all, more than once now, seemed like the most genuine of them.

Maybe it was the way he spoke about his wife?

Diane looked back at her again, but found she had to turn away. Not out of revulsion, but because one look at her had rattled Diane to her core. Like she was looking into the secrets of the universe. Strangely, she was not scared for herself, not really. But she was very scared for Brad. She could not stand the thought of losing him and for some reason, she felt like he was more at risk than her. Tears escaped her eyes as she thought about him. She started a little when Althea took her hand and squeezed it, Diane looked at her, pleading, hoping she had some kind of answer, she saw she was holding Desma's hand in her other, who was holding Jackie's hand in hers. Forming a chain with her, sisters supporting sisters.

Diane heard that voice in her head again, *Oh Diane, you have no idea how true that is, stand firm with these sisters of yours, and you will be fine. I will look after your brother.*

A crashing sound brought her back to herself when the reverend's brother was dropped unceremoniously to the ground. The giant looked out at the gathered family and spoke slowly and clearly.

"Enough with the threats and promises, let us move on so that you can make your preparations and honor your traditions. We have two more things to discuss tonight. The Choosing will occur on Sunday, two nights from now. Four of you will be chosen to join my bride and I on our mission. You need not fear, yes life will change. But the journey will be one of discovery and knowledge you cannot imagine, and your life will be given purpose beyond your wildest reckoning."

As he walked up and down in front of the pulpit like a practiced lecturer, he gazed out onto the congregation. He stopped and stared at Diane for a moment then looked down at her holding hands with Althea who held hands with Desma and her with Jackie. After a moment he leaped down in front of the four of them. Completely ignoring Judith and the other older woman seated at the end of the pew. "My love, you must come and see this for yourself."

Faster than Diane could see, the woman was next to him, holding his hand in her own. Even as big as she was her hand seemed like a delicate child's in his. What an endearingly intimate gesture, Diane thought to herself.

He knelt before the girls and spoke to the woman next to him. "My love would you look at this, there seems to have been a mistake, as there are wolves among these sheep, and grinned like he had just told the funniest joke in the world. I mean, there are Lewis among these Wilcothes. Not only that, but there are also Lewis twins, among them. Tell me, Desma, Althea." He nodded to each girl in turn. "How fares clan Lewis and what ever could you be doing here?"

Murmuring began in the congregation and Diane felt the slight shift in Althea, but the girl never released her hand. Althea bowed her head respectfully, then spoke in a clear voice.

"Father Stag and Mother Moon, we have come to fulfill our obligations to our mother's family."

Father Stag, Diane thought, *what an appropriate name for him. That is exactly perfect.* Diane had to lean her head back to keep from losing an eye when Father Stag bowed his head toward Althea, then he rose quickly to his feet.

"Ladies, your father's family is well known to me, and your integrity and courage are without question. You make your family proud and should hold your head high as always. Now to the next bit of business that I am afraid is not as pleasant."

At this Father Stag pointed over Diane's shoulder and said, "Melinda Wilcothe, will you come to the front of the church and join us?"

Judith spun around to look backward then back to the Stag with a look of open contempt, "You monster, she has been through enough, leave her be."

In a flash Mother Moon was on her, straddling her lap and pushing the much smaller woman's head back hard, holding her mouth shut. Diane was scared she would just pull Judith's head clean off.

"If you think for a moment that my husband's love for me is any greater than mine for him, I can promise you, you are mistaken. If you breathe one more word in my presence again. You will regret it."

In a blink, she was around the aisle and beckoning to a small brown-haired girl of maybe fourteen.

Father Stag spoke softly, but somehow powerfully at the same time. Like a whisper through a million speakers.

"Melinda, child, the time has come for your prayers to be answered, the God of your uncle does not hear the cries of the meek and oppressed. But I swear to you here and now on this sacred mountain, we do, and did, you only have a moment or two left of the hell created for you, and then you will be free to start your life anew. Do you understand me?"

The girl, looking scared, but accepting of her fate, nodded. "Good, my love, as loathe as I am to not have your touch, I am afraid, this sweet child will need a mother's love now even more than I."

At this, Mother Moon walked to the girl's side, reached down, and took her hand. Diane was again taken aback at the loving way those hands, which only a moment before seemed ready to rip Judith apart at the seams, now cradled the hand of a scared little girl.

"Melinda, child, where is your mother?" Father Stag's voice was low and even.

"She died four years ago when I was ten."

"For that, I am truly sorry, a daughter should know her mother's love for all her days. So, is it just you and your father? "

"Yes sir."

At this, he leaped back up to the pulpit and scooped up the reverend's brother who was still lying on the floor and sat him upright. Kneeling next to him he propped the man up in the sitting position. Like a man with a ventriloquist dummy.

"And this man, John Wilcothe, is your father?"

Father Stag sounded more like a trial lawyer at this point. Diane was confused, and as she looked around, she realized most everyone else was as well.

Only Reverend Wilcothe and his wife looked truly scared, and when she turned to Althea, she saw her and Desma both enrapt. Smiling wide like they were watching the best movie they had ever seen or seeing a great band. She squeezed Althea's hand, and the girl looked at her questioningly for only a moment before she mouthed.

"Justice." Diane did not understand any more than before. The voice in her head, so similar to her mother's but not quite right. *Now you will see the truth of who we are.*

Melinda nodded yes towards Father Stag and pushed herself closer to Mother Moon's side. "Melinda, where were you last year, why did you leave Alabama?"

"I was with my mom's family sir, I stayed with my mom's cousin in Michigan."

"Melinda, child, I swear to you, you are safe, no one can hurt you. You are in the arms of the most powerful woman to walk this earth. She is older than the trees around us and her love for innocent children is bigger than this mountain. Please tell us the truth, you have never met anyone in your mother's family before, have you?"

John Wilcothe finally came around and stared at his daughter, dazed for only a moment before speaking, "No, That's not true." His voice slurred a little as he tried to stand up. "Tell them Melinda, tell them, you stayed with your mom's cousin in Michigan."

A low growl issued from the throat of Father Stag.

Melinda was crying now, her voice trembling. "No, I won't lie for you, not here in God's house, not anymore."

"Bastard." yelled a solitary voice from the back,

"What did you do?" came another.

The reverend snapped his head up at the sounds. "Brothers and sisters please, we cannot be deceived, whatever it is these people are trying to accuse my brother of or bewitch his poor slow-witted daughter into saying. We cannot give in to this treachery. My brother has done nothing but try to raise his daughter the best way he can since her mother died and left them alone."

The Lewis twins rose as one and pushed their way out of the pew, over Diane, and into the aisle, where they stood side by side behind Mother Moon. The large woman looked up over her shoulder, unworried but curious. They bowed their heads in deference to the Mother Moon, on her knees holding tight to the scared Melinda. Diane suddenly understood. They are showing their solidarity with Father Stag and Mother Moon, they are offering their support for this scared little girl. Diane stood as well, and walked to the aisle, again taking her place next to Althea who did not look at her but reached for her hand again. She felt another hand on her shoulder and looked up to see Brad standing behind them, standing firm behind the group. Jackie slid out and stood next to Brad. The sound of shuffling clothes, and bodies shifting, told her they were not alone.

Melinda looked around at the growing group of people behind her and then back at Mother Moon, who whispered, "Just tell the truth child, no one can hurt you with your family behind you and me at your side. You are as safe as in your own mother's arms." Diane heard sobbing coming from the group behind her.

"After Mama died, Daddy started sleeping in my room with me, then he moved me into his room. He said he was lonely and needed me to keep him company like Mom used to. Last year, I got pregnant, and he didn't want anyone to know what he did, so he sent me away to this church, they kept me there until the baby was born, then took her away from me, and sent me back. He told me I had to tell everyone that I spent a year with my mom's family, or he would get into trouble for what he did, and he promised to never touch me again. But he lied."

"Rot in hell, John."

"You sick pervert, how could you."

"Hang the bastard"

The voices were getting louder from all over the church.

On the stage, John was crying and shaking his head over and over. Reverend Wilcothe had left the stage and stood next to his wife, who just stared blankly at her brother-in-law.

Father Stag stood the man up, holding onto the collar of his jacket. "John, speak now, will you defend yourself? Can you defend yourself? Did you do what your daughter is accusing you of, did you use your position, as her father, her protector, her only living parent? Did you hurt this child, abuse her, for your own gratification?"

John was blubbering, "It wasn't like that, not like that, she didn't understand, she just kept hugging me and holding on to me."

At this, Althea screamed, a primal, painful sound. Everyone except her twin fell back from her, Diane stumbled into the pew next to her and looked up directly into the eyes of Mother Moon, tears ran down her cheeks. Her tattoos started to shimmer as if possessed of their own inner light. Althea continued her primal screaming. Diane did not understand how she could maintain that sound, that intensity, for that long. The church broke out into chaos. one of the men that Brad had been sitting next to before he rose to join the group in the aisle, jumped two rows of pews, and darted for the stage. He was intercepted by another of the older members of the church just before he made the stage. Father Stag looked at him puzzled and smiled.

Althea's scream grew even louder, more fierce, Diane could feel a vibration that seemed to center on Althea and radiate from her, it was a feeling of pure rage. Even Brad, behind the Lewis girls was shaking and red faced with anger. And had taken no mind of his sister falling; and was solely focused on the big man in the suit who had just admitted to raping his daughter and getting her pregnant.

Had that bastard really just tried to blame it on her?

She could feel the rage being slammed through every cell in her body, she recognized it for what it was, but it did not seem to affect her like everyone else.

Then it stopped. The entire church fell into silence when Althea went quiet. Everyone was staring at Father Stag and John Wilcothe. Wilcothe was mumbling incoherently.

Father Stag spoke again. "I know that this has been a long and trying night for all of you, and the coming days will be difficult. Our intentions in unearthing this atrocity have not been to sew discord among you, although I urge you to look closely at those among you who still stand in defense of this admitted monster, this defiler of innocence. The purpose was to illustrate to you the importance of protecting innocence and rooting out those who would use their positions of trust and authority to harm those who cannot defend themselves. What comes next will be unpleasant, and I understand some of you will be made very uncomfortable. But you must stand witness, you must remember every horrid detail as a ward against allowing this evil to take root among your family ever again. Melinda, your father is going to pay for his crimes against you. He is going to pay for violating your trust and using your grief as a means to gratify his own desires. You are the one person I would excuse from watching what comes next, you have suffered so much, and I do not wish you to come to further harm. If you like, I will spirit you somewhere safe and you can spend the rest of your life surrounded by a loving family never seeing what became of your father. Or you can stay and witness his just and fair end. I leave it up to you."

Melinda pulled away from the Mother Moon just enough to stand up straight. She looked into the eyes of the man about to punish her father for what he did to her, this giant supernatural being, who looked every moment more and more like the angel the voice in Diane's head, claimed he was.

"I will stay sir, but I would very much like it if Mother Moon could keep holding my hand through it. I will be afraid, and I feel very safe with her."

Father Stag stepped slowly and deliberately off of the pulpit and stood before the girl.

"My child, I am afraid Mother Moon will be preoccupied, you see, hers is the hand of justice for the oppressed, I am merely her consort and lover for all of eternity. Would it be ok, if I held your hand while she does what must be done and we can stand here with these valiant friends and cousins of yours, and together we will all be safe from those among us who hurt the innocent."

He reached for Melinda, and she released the hand of Mother Moon, who smiled up at her husband, Diane could see in that smile a love that she suddenly craved very badly, she wanted to know what it was like to have someone as devoted to you as the Father Stag appeared to be to the Mother Moon. Mother Moon moved quickly toward the stage as John Wilcothe began backing up, the reverend Wilcothe stepped in front of her, his hands up in a gesture of peace and as one asking for a reprieve.

"Please, I ask of you, the grace and mercy shown to all sinners through the blood of our Lord Jesus, my brother may have sinned, and surely he should stand in God's judgment, but we cannot just execute him, there are laws of man, and God's law demands repentance and forgiveness so that he be admitted into heaven. "

"Sit down reverend."

The voice came not from Mother Moon staring him down or even her husband but from Desma Lewis. She was calm, but the look on her face was pure murder, and she said it again.

"Sit down Reverend, all here witnessed your brother's admission, one way or another, he will be punished for his crime. If not by them, then my sister will finish what she started, and this congregation will rip him apart and you, if you attempt to stop them."

The voice in Diane's head spoke again, *You have allied yourself with powerful friends child, I cannot wait to see what you all can accomplish together, now watch, and learn what becomes of men who prey upon the weak when our justice comes for them.*

John Wilcothe stopped pleading and began yelling, "You cannot do this, my Lord and Savior Jesus Christ will not allow one of his faithful servants to fall to some devil bitch, Ye though I walk through the valley of the shadow of death, I shall fear no ev."

The word cut off as Mother Moon jumped the last ten feet from the floor to the area in front of the baptismal tank behind the pulpit where John had backed up. She grabbed the back of his head and kissed him hard on the mouth, his body stiffened violently like he was trying to pull away from her. She then jumped backward, easily covering the distance from where she was, to alight softly on the carpet in front of Melinda and Father Stag. John Wilcothe screamed in agony as his body rolled into a ball, every joint in his body contracting at once, just a little tighter than it was supposed to. Then violently, he straightened as every joint overextended. Diane heard a popping sound as he drew in a breath to start screaming again, then rolled even tighter into a ball before, his back cracked as he was pulled further into the contraction than it could handle. Then snap, back out to hyperextension. Even his jaw stretched, his fingers were splayed out at forty-five degrees past where the joints and tendons should have stopped them but did not. Diane looked at the Lewis twins and Brad then over to Father Stag, who was now holding Melinda tight against his chest. Her head rested on his massive torso as she watched her father tortured to death with the same eyes Diane used to see in pictures of the kids in concentration camps or working in the coal mines.

Diane could not imagine the pain this girl had been through. Wilcothe's final scream as his back extended so far back his head touched his heels, drew her back to the spectacle of his death. With a final snap, his spine severed, and the screaming stopped, although his body continued its cycle of contraction and extension.

Father Stag turned and spoke to the congregation. "It is done. When John Wilcothe's body has pulled itself apart, he will need to be burned. Reverend Wilcothe, you and your wife will oversee that process, alone. That will atone for your transgression of attempting to interfere with my bride as she went about her sacred duties, unless my love, you would rather come up with a more creative punishment for the Reverend." Another sickening crunch as John Wilcothe's body continued ripping itself apart and someone in the back moaned and hit the floor. Father Stag kissed Melinda on the top of the head. "It is time for someone to take this child, she is tired and needs love. Who in your family will see to her well-being and care?"

A middle-aged woman in the back walked forward, "I'd be happy to look after her, do you remember me, sweetheart, I used to come round your Ma's when you were little and help her out with housework and such. I have no kids of my own but would be happy to have you for as long as you would want to stay, your dear mother was a good friend to me when my Paul passed on so young, and I would be happy to repay the kindness she showed me, to her own kinfolk."

Melinda nodded her head and whispered something in the ear of Father Stag, so great was his size compared to her, she almost looked like a toddler in his arms and not a girl of fourteen years. He sat her down and she squeezed his hand one last time, only flinching a little at the sound of her father's corpse finally coming apart at the seams and coming to rest.

"Then our business here is concluded for the night. We will return at the appointed time two days from now. When we do, we will choose the four among us who will join us on our journey. Remember, all here must be in attendance on that night." At that, both he and Mother Moon faded from view.

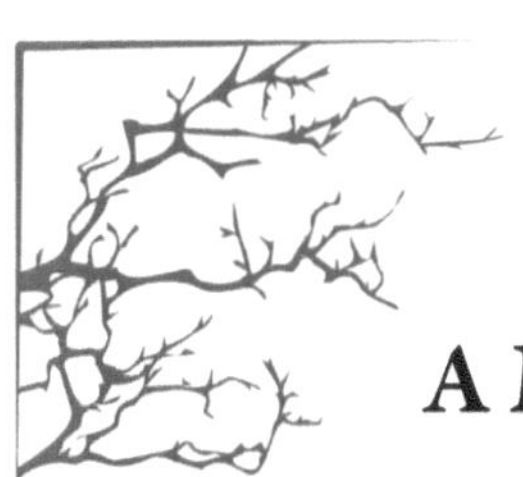

A Mother's Love

"Althea, please tell me what in the world is going on?"

Diane, along with all the other girls had been rushed, by Judith and a couple of the other church elders, from the small chapel, into an annex building at the back of the church.

It looked like a small cafeteria or meeting hall, mats, cots, and pallets had been cast about the floor as well as hanging racks and some small tables. The men were rushed out the other side of the church presumably toward the barn at the front of the property, Diane attempted to talk to Brad and Althea had pulled her away as they were herded like cattle.

"When things calm down; after we have eaten and the church elders leave us for the evening, Desma and I will do our best to explain the truth of what you have seen tonight. For now, we are safe, stay close to Desma and me. Even these zealots will not harm you out of respect for our father's family, as you witnessed, even among the most powerful and revered beings in all creation, our family is known and looked upon with favor."

From behind her Jackie spoke up, "About that."

Althea cut her off, "Jackie, I promise, when we can rid ourselves of the church elders and only those who may be chosen are here, my sister will explain, as best she can, what is happening. But let's not cause any undue stress. We are all tired and emotional, many of these people here just watched a beloved member of their congregation ripped apart by what they think of as demons. To tell them now, that their entire belief structure is false and everything they have been taught by everyone they know and respect is a lie, would be cruel and antagonistic. Let us eat and settle in, my sister Desma is a fantastic storyteller, and just as I have the gift to enrage and incite, Desma has the gift to calm and subdue. Watching her tell the old stories is one of my favorite things in the world."

With this Althea led the group over to where the rest had gathered, fifteen or so were milling around a small area set up with wooden cafeteria tables and metal folding chairs. Several women from the church were laying out lunch meat and vegetables along with condiments, some pies, and a tray of cookies.

As the four approached most all the other women turned and took notice. Diane was not comfortable with the scrutiny at all, but she saw Jackie puff her chest out a little and the twins seemed not to notice at all. She imagined they were used to people staring at this point in their lives. Not only were identical twins, not something you see every day, but these twins, with their height, and their skin, without blemish, and as pale as a Greek statue, were a jarring sight.

That is of course without mentioning the fact that Father Stag had called them out of the crowd. Wolves among the sheep, or Lewis among the Wilcothes, she thought to herself. She could not get that out of her head, Desma's smile as she mouthed "Justice." The look on both twins' faces were as if they were seeing something they had been waiting their whole life for.

Within a few moments, the food was laid out. The church elders were lingering when Desma spoke up.

"Sisters of the Red Mountain Pentecost Revival, it is time for you to take your leave, you who cannot be chosen will allow us our preparations and meditations."

Two of the women began grabbing up their things, and the third stood stubbornly staring at Desma.

A small voice from a side table. "Sister Paige, you heard Ms. Lewis, this is our time, please leave us."

Everyone in the room stared at Melinda Wilcothe. Diane gasped, the girl appeared so young and had just admitted to a room full of people, strangers, and known alike that she had been abused by her father, impregnated, and sent away to give up the child for adoption. Then watched her father torn apart as punishment.

Now here she was, seeming revitalized and somehow more present than Diane could have imagined, chastising an elder from the church where she spent most of her life. Diane shook her head in disbelief, this could not get any stranger. As the girls settled in for dinner, Desma walked to the corner of the room and turned off most of the lights in the small room. Several girls cast odd and suspicious looks her way.

She walked to the front of the room and spoke. "Sisters, if you will permit me, and give me just a few minutes of your attention, I would like to tell you a story. A long time ago, before this modern era, a woman was taken from her home as a child bride. She was, you see, the only daughter of a poor goat farmer, but just like her mother, who had passed away in childbirth, she had a knack for divining. She did not know how, but she could toss bones and stones and see signs of storms coming, she could tell men's fortunes, she could find water with remarkable accuracy. She could also stare into a flame and predict the coming of the seasons. With time the young girl gained a bit of notoriety, some folks around her province even came with gifts for her family for her to help divine the weather or come to their property and find the perfect spot for digging a well."

Diane was sitting with her eyes closed, she realized that she could see, images in her mind, like a movie playing on the back of her eyelids, a flash of an open field, an older man, tending a flock, and a young girl, her dark skin shining with the sweat of effort as she carried buckets of water toward a small structure.

Desma continued "Her and her father lived a peaceful life on their little farm. Then one day, the farmer came. He arrived dressed in finery like the village had never seen. He first inquired about her ability, her father, a kind, but not overly bright man, was proud of his one and only daughter and her growing renown. So as fathers are prone to do, when talking about their children, be bragged, about her abilities, her beauty, her charm. So much had he boasted and bragged about his daughter, that by the time she arrived home from her daily chores to find her father in their small house entertaining this stranger, the farmer had already made up his mind. He would marry the girl."

At this Desma reached for her cup of water and took a drink, Diane looked around the room, no one was moving, no one stirred. She realized she could not remember when she had last taken a breath.

Desma began again. "The girl, Niri, was distraught, she did not want to marry this farmer, she did not want to leave the land where she and all her mothers before her, had been born. Who would look after her father? But the farmer insisted, and offered a great dowry, enough that her father could find help, or perhaps a wife for himself. He had just inherited a large farm and estate from his recently passed father and would guarantee a yearly stipend for her father as well, in grain and livestock.

Niri saw no way out, her father had dedicated his life to her, while many men would have been angry at not having a son or would have immediately taken another wife and tried to have sons, her father remained committed to giving her the best life he could. He never once was bitter or angry in her presence. Kind and loving and devoted to his daughter, she felt like not agreeing to this, and denying him this opportunity and forcing him to continue to support her as she aged would be selfish and no way to repay his love. So, in the spring of that year, she loaded her few belongings into the largest and finest cart she had ever seen and traveled to her new home and new husband. The farmer was extremely kind, he welcomed her to his large home, even giving her a room of her home until they would be wed the following month, and a serving girl, Tuniby, to see to her needs as she prepared to be married. She was given full privilege over all the home and land and was given the choice to oversee the packing of the dowry to be shipped to her father on the day they were to be wed. Not one for idleness, Niri relished the chance to have a task and to get to know some of the people working on her new husband's farm.

The workers on the farm were poor, from a neighboring village and Niri found she had much in common with them, more in fact than with her betrothed. Although he was a handsome man, tall and strong, with piercing, intelligent eyes, and skin as dark as the night sky. She noticed his skin was also absent any blemishes or scars, and in the evenings when they walked together and she took his hand into hers, she found not a single callus or blister, only a slight rougher patch in the crook of his middle knuckle. From holding a writing quill, but not from a day in the fields. Still, he seemed kind and willing to allow her to keep her traditions as well as allowing her contact with her father. When the yearly shipment went to her father's village she would accompany it, and spend the week with him, before returning with the wagons. Unless of course, she was too far along with child to travel, which he admitted with a wide smile and charming bow, that he hoped she would be often as he prayed every day to his God for many sons. Not only to help grow his family but to aid in overseeing and growing his farm and property. You see, he dreamed of one day being the wealthiest man in their province, and to do that he would need many sons, and he had no doubt she would provide these for him, as his God always answered the prayers of the faithful.

Niri did not question this logic, although her people had no knowledge of the farmer's God, they prayed to the spirits of the land and air and water. They did not believe there was a single holy creator in charge of all manner of men's affairs but a pervasive unity that connects all creation. This unity was presented as many faces and spirits, including personifications of creation, as well as her ancestors. She would kneel in the morning and face the sun and pray to the spirits of the sky, thanking them for the warmth and light of the sun, and in the evening when her mind was quiet, she would ask her mother and grandmother to guide her hands to make food that would nourish her and her father. But she also knew in her heart she was praying to the same thing."

Diane was amazed at the vividness of the visions dancing in her mind, she opened her eyes and glanced around the room. Althea was sitting cross-legged on the floor in front of the table counter where Desma sat, cradling little Melinda's head in her lap. The younger girl had a serene look on her face and was enjoying the story as much as Diane herself was. Jackie sat to Diane's left and had been resting her head on her shoulder. All around the room Diane saw that the girls and women had settled in, many of them sitting or lying close to one another. One of the older girls had taken her hair down and it cascaded over her shoulders in dark brown waves as two younger girls brushed it out.

Desma's voice overtook her mind again, weaving its spell. "Niri did not wish to upset her future husband, trying to mind the lessons from her serving girl, that men of this province, and specifically men who had abandoned the old teachings and embraced the idea of a single God, did not suffer women to question their wisdom. But she could not shake the idea that if God answered the wishes of all faithful men, then what happened when two faithful men prayed for the opposite things? Would that not mean that God would have to leave one of their prayers unanswered? It did not seem like a question her husband would want to answer or even think about."

"Soon enough the day of the wedding arrived, a holy man came from the nearby village and gave Niri the lines that she would need to recite to be married in the eyes of her husband's God. No such thing existed among her people, and she did not like the way the words felt in her mouth, words like dutiful, submissive, meek, and obedient did not sit well on her spirit. Those were the words used to describe children and livestock, not a wife and mother of your children. But she agreed to wear the veil and recite the words if it would make the farmer happy and in turn make her father happy and bring her and her future children a peaceful household."

"The morning of the ceremony, Niri looked into the leaves of her tea and saw a bleak sign indeed, a burning home. She called for her serving girl and asked for one of the meat birds to be brought to the garden outside her private chambers. When the servant brought the bird Niri took from her bags a small knife, two bowls, and a small platter. She locked the door and asked Tuniby to watch over her and assure that she was not disturbed as she was going to consult the spirits to help her interpret the sign. There should have been favorable signs over her wedding, she was doing the right thing for everyone, how could that not be favored by all the spirits and ancestors?"

"Niri stripped from her morning gown and knelt in the dirt, the platter and two bowls in front of her and the meat bird held firmly in her hands and raised her eyes to the sky. She prayed to the spirit of her ancestors for guidance and thanked the spirit of the bird for its gift of sight and food. She then opened the throat of the bird and held it tightly over the first bowl. When it was drained, she painted the symbol that represented her mother onto her forehead and then with one smooth movement of the blade opened the stomach of the bird, reached in pulled out its innards, and dropped them in one pile in the other bowl. She laid the empty and drained carcass on the platter and stared deeply into the bowl of organs and intestines. She let her vision go blurry and waited until she felt the presence of her ancestors then focused on the bloody pile. She bowed her head, having seen her answer and now she needed only to figure out how best to use her knowledge to prevent disaster."

"The wedding ceremony was indeed beautiful, flowers and music and a garment the likes of which she had never imagined. Her groom lavished her with jewelry and gifts. She danced and ate and sang, she very much wished her father could have attended, she did not think about her mother as one might think. She felt, in her heart of hearts that perhaps her mother did not approve or was trying to send her a warning of some sort. At the end of the ceremony, after the last of the guests had said their congratulations and bestowed their gifts on the couple, her husband rose, took her by the hand, and began to lead her down the aisle toward the main house. A cheer went up from the revelers, Niri knew what was to come next but knew also what the spirits had told her and needed to navigate these next few minutes carefully."

"When they arrived in his chamber, he held her close, professing her beauty and his undying love for her. All of this she enjoyed greatly, sex was not taboo among her people and while she had not experienced it fully yet, she was very much looking forward to many years of pleasure at the hands of this handsome man. She had read the signs, she knew, if she became with child tonight, she would not bear him a son. Not only would their first child be a daughter, but all their children would be daughters. They would have no sons if she could not wait until the next new moon to become pregnant. As she tried to think of how to tell him, he kissed down her neck and ran his fingertips up her rib cage. Her body reacted and her skin flushed, and she reached back and held his head tight against her neck, encouraging him.

Niri was wise in her years; and understood the signs and the importance of heeding such warnings. She was also young, and excited, and very much in love. Her concerns fell away with her dress, and her warnings to her new husband joined his clothes on the floor and all thoughts of anything but pleasure became a problem for another day."

Diane shifted in her chair uncomfortably warm and very aware of the heat of Jackie's body against hers as they sat pressed against one another. The vision of Niri's wedding night was clear and graphic, and Diane knew she should be ashamed of the things racing through her mind right now, about herself and the woman resting her head on her shoulder. But mostly about Althea, naked and bold. Braver and more daring than anyone she had ever imagined. She did not understand what was happening, but what she did understand, was that even with all that had happened in the few hours she had been here, right now, in this room, with these women, she felt more comfortable, more herself than she ever had before. She glanced up at Althea who was smiling at her with a thoughtful look while Melinda appeared to sleep in her lap.

Diane smiled back and Jackie whispered in her ear. "I am not sure if she thinks you're pretty or thinks you would make a pretty handbag."

Diane gave her a light elbow in the ribs and looked up at Desma who seemed to be looking somewhere in the space above most of the girls in the room.

"As was foretold, soon Niri's belly grew heavy with child, and she gave birth to their first girl. Her husband was dutiful and caring, even allowing her to send for one of her childhood friends to come and stay with them as a midwife and nurse to Niri and the child, Dinuyea. Niri sent word with the first wagon of supplies, sent to her father as per their agreement. She knew her father could not read but that someone in the village would read it to him, naming her daughter and sending him her many blessings along with the yearly payment. The relationship with her husband had been wonderful so far. He taught her the administration of the farm, record keeping, paying the workers, and collecting living payments from the people who lived in small homes on his large property. When they were done with the day's work, they dined together every evening, him recounting tales of his travels and schooling and her telling stories passed down from her mother's people, of great spirits and heroes. Every night, he took her into their bed, and they made love until her body, growing larger every day made it difficult. Even then he lavished her with long baths and rubbed her swollen belly with oils she made. It was everything she had hoped a marriage would be and none of the things she had been told to expect. But now that their daughter had been born, she could feel the difference in him, and it was only then that she remembered what she read in the leaves and guts. As her body healed and Tuniby and Binlai, her midwife and nurse, cared for her and her daughter, she began to feel more fearful. If her husband was just processing and learning to live with his disappointment, she could understand that. As kind as he is and smart and caring, having sons was still incredibly important to him. How might he react when no matter how many times they tried they could not have a son? Would he send her away, she did not know what his laws allowed, would he kill her so he could remarry, she did not think he was capable of it, but the cruelty of men when their ego is challenged, can be without limit."

"As you may guess, it was not long before her husband called her to him and demanded, more forcefully than she was used to, that she rejoin him sleeping in their marriage bed and allow Binlai and Tuniby to tend to Dinuyea so that she could return to her marital duties and bear him a son. There was no tenderness in his request, no longing or lust, just duty, he would have a son, and she would fulfill that request."

"Before long, Niri was once again with child, this time, as soon as Binlai had confirmed the pregnancy her husband announced during dinner that she would be returning to the nursery. Niri implored her husband to allow her to stay close to him, declaring her love and affection. He would not hear it, she could prove her love for him by providing him with a son, someone to carry his name, someone to help with his farm. It did not matter that she had taken on many of his duties and continued well into her pregnancies with them. It seemed, for some reason, her only value in his eyes had become her ability to provide him with a son. She did not know what had changed in his eyes, but she knew that this child would also be a daughter, and she was scared he would get worse, but she had no one to blame but herself. She ignored the signs, the message from the spirits and her ancestors, and now she must pay the price. She only hoped she could keep her daughters safe."

"Years passed and the signs remained true, after five years of marriage Niri had given birth to three daughters, Dinuyea, Tanas, and Wicoyte. When Wicoyte was barely weaned, her husband came to her again, demanding she move back into the marriage bed. With every passing year and every daughter born his demeanor grew colder. He no longer allowed Niri to work on the farm, handling the accounts and payroll. She may not have been allowed to work on the accounts, but she could see the farm, and with each passing season the output of the farm decreased."

"After the birth of Wicoyte, her husband brought a midwife from the neighboring village, J'ineele. He told Niri and Binlai that he thought a local midwife might be able to ensure him a son. Both women scoffed at the idea in private, and in truth J'ineele, was rarely around, she did not assist Niri in any significant way, nor did she help with the other children. It did not take Niri or Binlai long to figure out the woman was not there for Niri or to assist with her pregnancy. Niri might not be out on the farm every day, but Binlai had made several friends among the workers and had even taken a couple of the farm hands as lovers as well as one of the washerwomen. All around the farm was the talk of the new woman the farmer had brought from town, and how she left her quarters every night supposedly to check on Niri. But was always seen leaving the farmer's chambers in the morning."

"Niri and Binlai knew what this meant and knew also that it could spell disaster for her and her daughters. She was not scared to be put out, she would return with her daughters to her father's village and make a life there for them. She knew her father would welcome them with open arms and while they would have a harder life than growing up on a wealthy farm, they would be loved and safe. She worried that because of his pride, he might try to harm them or somehow blame her for his want to separate and she did not know if his customs allowed for that kind of separation or if she would need to be dead for him to be absolved of his guilt. She made up her mind, that after this child was born, surely to be a daughter, Niri would send

Binlai back to their village with her father's yearly stipend to see if arrangements could be made for them back there in secret. Once Binlai returned, she would petition her husband. Let her take their daughters and return to her home. They would trouble him no more. She would seek no compensation, and he could find a wife that would provide him with the sons he so wanted and deserved. She felt like if she played to his ego and kept the guilt on herself, she might have a chance to escape with their lives at the least."

Her audience silent and enrapt, Desma continued. "After the birth of her fourth daughter, Millin, Niri approached her husband, he was cold and distant but agreeable when she asked if Binlai could accompany her father's stipend to send word to him about her well-being and the birth of her latest child. As well as bring any word from her village as she had grown homesick and hoped that some word from home might help her. The shipment departed on time and Binlai was on the lead carriage, although seeing them off, Niri could not help but notice that the stipend seemed much smaller than was previously agreed upon. But she said nothing, now was the time for waiting and planning, not the time for arousing the suspicions or anger of her husband. After three weeks had gone by, Niri was missing Binlai terribly, not only her company, but also her help, nursing a newborn while looking after three other small children was no easy task, and of course, J'ineele was never around."

"Many times, Niri had tried to send word to her husband that she needed help, through the servants that brought food and linens, but no help came. Almost five weeks after Binlai's departure on a trip that should have taken no more than ten days, Niri was up late into the night nursing Millin when she heard a shuffling in the hallway outside her door. A click and a rush of cool night air, and Binlai stood before her, wrapped in a gown and head scarf that Niri did not recognize. Binlai told her how on the road just outside of the village the driver of the carriage attacked her, he attempted to strangle her. She only got away because he was fat and slow and she was able to twist away from him before he got his hands around her neck, she jumped off the carriage and took off through the night. After many days of travel, she arrived at their village only to find that Niri's father's farm was abandoned, the neighbors told her that shortly after Niri left, they found the farm empty and a note saying he had gone to live on the big farm with his daughter. Niri knew this could not be so, her father could not read or write; and would have never left his ancestral home, not even for her."

"Niri asked about the yearly supply drops, and the villagers told Binlai that there had never been a single wagon arrive, not even the first year. It was then that Binlai suspected that the carriage driver had tried to kill her because he and Niri's husband would know that she would figure out the truth and tell Niri. But because no one ever came looking for her, she suspected that the carriage driver had lied and told the farmer that she was dead. She worked her way back across the countryside, laying low and being careful not to be seen. She stopped at a farm a half a day's journey from here and made friends with a couple of the farm hands, reading their palms in exchange for a meal and a soft bed. Over the evening meal, they told her how the farmer from the big farm down the road had come recently and told the two brothers who owned their farm that his wife was very ill and not likely to make it through the next season. She had been fostering four little girls, he would happily trade these little girls for the two brothers to have as servants or wives, whatever they wanted, in exchange for some livestock. So that was that, she was not ill at all, but all the pieces to the puzzle added up, her husband, the man she so loved, had decided that she would not live through the next season, and he was selling their daughters, his own flesh and blood, for some cattle. She would not allow it, she would sneak to his room and kill him in his sleep, him and that J'ineele, she had no doubt that woman was at the root of this. She would slaughter them both and run with their girls. She talked with Binlai through the night and into the next morning. Finally exhausted, they lay in each other's arms and slept."

"In her fitful sleep Niri dreamed she was walking with her daughters in a lush green forest. She had never seen such trees, birds, and flowers; they followed a running stream of the clearest water she had ever seen and when they passed into a clearing she found a host of women there. Old and young, women of all races, in dress and styles that she could not even imagine. At the head of this host stood her mother. Who held out her arms wide to her. She ran to her mother and embraced her, crying, she turned her head to tell her daughters to come and meet their grandmother. She was so excited to be able to see her mother hold them; and shower them with the love and affection she so desperately needed from her."

"But instead of her daughters, she saw only a barren landscape. Only moments ago, where her daughters were running barefoot through green grasses and splashing in cold clear water, now there was only dust and ash. She turned back to face her mother, and behind her the landscape was just as barren and wasted except instead of a host of women, there were, as far as the eyes could see, men, in the armaments of battle, in the robes of holy men, farmers and tenders, all carrying whips and chains and weapons, that seemed pulled from the imagination of children. Her mother whispered in her ear, *"It is time my child, time for you to choose, the world you want for your daughters and their daughters. When you wake, you have a choice, continue as you are, at the mercy of your husband, and hope that you can reason with his bruised ego and injured pride, so that he does not sell your daughters into slavery as he would sell cattle. Or follow the path that will be opened for you.* Niri cried in her mother's arms, she wanted so badly to find a way to save her daughters, she wept for them, she wept for all the daughters of the world, pushed, and shoved, abused, and treated like slaves and cattle. The girls were given to old men for pleasure, the wives beaten and bred until their bodies could take no more, the girls serving and cleaning and never seeing their dreams come true.

Her mother spoke again, *Niri, you can change the fate of our daughters, you can change the fate of so many daughters, give them a home, a place where they may grow and prosper. But first, you must keep them safe, and to do that, you must remember our ways, you must call upon the spirits and your ancestors for help. She slipped a piece of paper into Niri's robe. Follow these instructions, follow them exactly, and then decide for yourself what is right. But always remember, I know that I was not there for you, but I always love you and would not have raised you to be breeding stock for this man, and I know your sweet father would not have wanted that either.*

Niri woke knowing in her heart what needed to be done, the dream had given her renewed purpose, she wished only that she had looked at the instructions, she felt there must have been something there that would have told her how to begin. But still, she knew now more than ever what she must do."

Desma stood up from her seat with her glass, it was hard to tell but to Diane, it seemed like she had been talking for hours. There was something about her voice, soft and musical, and the way that her storytelling seemed to paint pictures on Diane's eyelids. It was mesmerizing. Diane's eyes shot open wide as it dawned on her, the exact opposite of Althea's scream in the chapel. Her voice made everyone enraged, if Mother Moon had not dealt with the reverend's brother, she was sure he would have been torn apart by the congregation. Twins, one with a voice capable of creating peace in your mind, the other rage. She wondered; would Althea's voice create the same kind of imagery if she had been describing something while invoking that rage. She wanted to ask her but could not think of a way to just blurt that out across a crowded room. There was something about these twins that made her feel both emboldened and incredibly conscious of just how small and limited her world had been up until now. She did not think they were much older than her, maybe a year, or two at most but they seemed like they understood something, like they had seen something that made them wiser and more capable than their age would suggest.

Diane scanned the room, the linoleum floor was spotless but aged, the walls were painted cinderblock and the drop ceiling looked fairly new. She turned back to Desma, awaiting the next part of her story. Desma stretched her back and took another sip of water.

Just as she began to speak a crash came from across the room as the doors to the hall slammed open. "You will not speak another word of those blasphemous lies in this holy place."

Judith was practically screeching as she ran into the room at the head of a group of about ten people from the church, the three women who had been laying the food out when they got into the hall, plus a few other random men and women that Diane could not name. Two of the men charged Desma and dragged her roughly from her spot, Althea, Diane, and Jackie all jumped up and more church members started grabbing at them.

Diane felt her hair being pulled hard and tried to turn to fight off whoever had grabbed her, but they were dragging her by the hair toward the door. Diane heard a loud pop and when she turned toward the sound Althea was being dragged, seemingly unconscious, by her legs toward the doors as well.

Judith was shrieking now, "We cannot allow these outsiders, these corrupt and evil whores, to mingle with the pure and sacred women of our congregation. We may not be able to interfere with the choosing, but we will not allow their blasphemy and witchcraft to soil our faith and foundation." At that, she grabbed Melinda Wilcothe by the hair and began dragging her screaming after the crowd. "And you, your lack of faith cost your father his life, you will not be allowed to poison this holy ground one moment longer."

Desma, Diane, Jackie, Althea, and Melinda were dragged out into the darkness.

Love, Boundless and Eternal

Twenty miles away from The Red Mountain Pentecost Revival, a small white cottage was nestled into the side of the mountain. No visible roads or trails leading to the house, nor can one see an obvious entrance. Two steps lead up to a small porch where one would expect to find a front door, but here there is only a window, a small, four-paned square with a blue flower box, filled with the yellow blossoms of the poisonous Cardosanto plant. Gorgeous, but not native to Alabama, nor easy to grow here.

Looking around the cottage reveals only more and more windows, of all shapes and sizes, round portcullis, bay windows, small peep windows, clear windows, painted windows, and stained glass. Every size, color, and geometric configuration one would imagine is represented on one or the other of the three sides that don't butt right up against the woods of the mountain. If there is an entrance to this home it is not one that we can ascertain, but there is smoke rolling from the chimney, surely someone knows a way in.

On the floor in front of the fireplace on a pile of furs and blankets lies The Stag, his name, the name he prefers is Seanchara, it's the name his creator calls him, but he is known by many names and accepts them. Lord Seanchara, The Harvester,

The Keeper of Paths, The Great Horned One, Cernunnos, and yes, once a generation he is known as the Stag of Red Mountain. He is currently lying naked, and although he seems smaller than the last time we saw him, he is still larger than any man. He also seems to be missing his great helm of antlers. At his side, her head on his broad, hairy chest, lay his bride. She has also gone by many names, many of which are lost to time and few of which she accepts. Currently, she is known as Elder Valkyrie, Bride of the Eternal, The First Light, and here in this place alongside her beloved Seanchara, she is the Mother Moon.

They do not know who is older, they remember, there was a time when they were adversaries, never meeting in direct combat, but more like two caged animals snarling through the bars at each other. Only when released, they ran to one another's arms for comfort rather than a fight to the death, and there they have remained ever since. But they serve different roles, and these obligations sometimes keep them apart for years and even when they don't, their time is fleeting, private, and never long enough. But here, at the time of the choosing on Red Mountain, where they select four from the Wilcothe clan to join the ranks of their home, they come to this place that Seanchara built for her; and that she maintains through her considerable magic. Here they are not only ancient and powerful beings. Here they are husband and wife, lovers lost in a rolling abandon. Here they sometimes stay for a month or more prior to The Choosing, so they may live as a couple. Every day they cook and eat together, every day they walk barefoot through the trees and commune with the forest around them. At night Seanchara will read her poetry and songs, some modern, some in languages lost for a millennium. They make love endlessly, sometimes on this pile of furs before the fire, sometimes under the heavens, and sometimes they drift into the stars so that all eternity can witness their passion.

Tonight Seanchara, lying contently, can feel his bride's tears as they roll down her ancient and beautiful cheeks and land softly on his chest. He knows why she is silently weeping. Their time is ending, in a day's time the choosing will be complete, and they will return to their duties. She, an Elder of Mercer, and he its guardian, neither has any idea of when they may be able to steal away like this again, outside of this meeting a generation from now. He knows, as any thoughtful lover would, why his love is crying at what should be a time of peace and joy, and like a thoughtful lover he does not ask her what is wrong.

"My love, I cannot remember the last time that the answer of who will be chosen is not immediately apparent. We have always struggled to find four worthy candidates from this family. Here we have more than enough to choose from."

The Mother Moon rolled over to face her lover, her arms crossed on his chest and her chin resting on the back of her hands. "The Lewis twins, seem obvious, already in touch with the lore and gifted well beyond their peers. What else do you see?"

"Not a surprise at all. The Lewis family is always one way or another. Either gifted witches from birth, even before crossing the veil, or absolute scoundrels. Interesting to see the twins seemed to both be the first. Probably good for all of us, did you see how quickly she brought the congregation to a boil?"

He stroked his fingers lightly up and down her spine, enjoying the way the skin prickled beneath them. "The Whistler siblings have potential, and I think a brother and sister would be beneficial, of course, a life in Mercer might be the best for young Melinda. But she has a lot of spiritual wounds to recover from and may not be ready to begin for many years. Two more of the young men, Paul, and his cousin Marcus, show much promise, Marcus is considering medical school, and Paul wants to go to law school. A doctor and a lawyer, every parent's dream, isn't that right Mother?"

She rolled her blue eyes at him, an endearing and mundane gesture. The kind of look that countless wives across countless ages have given to their husbands when they were getting too clever for their own good. In this moment he felt like he could stare into those beautiful blue eyes for eternity, and of all the Father's creations, it was he who understood what that meant better than any. She smiled up at him, "Seanchara, do you ever see a time, a time when you and I are no longer necessary? A time when we can spend our days together instead of running the width and breadth of the world saving the innocent and protecting the witches of Mercer as they continue their mission."

"Are you asking me if I ever see a time when the strong will not oppress the weak or predators will not prey? I do not. Can I imagine a time when others may take our place? I have wondered myself for many years. But who is there, that can see into the hearts and minds of all who may enter Mercer? Who but you could guide the Elders of Mercer on their mission? Is it delusion or an inflated sense of self-importance that leads me to believe we are necessary to the mission of Mercer? We are unique in the universe, my love, there are no other two beings like us. While we may be from different origins, we have that in common, and I cannot help but believe that our story has yet to see its end. I dream, when I allow myself that luxury, of a life at your side.

Not just these fleeting moments, but a real life at your side. In my weakest moments, I have cried to the Father for relief, for respite, so that we can live our life together. Always my prayers must go unanswered. Always the cries of the innocent drown out my desires."

The Mother Moon crawled across his massive body, straddling him, and snuggling her face into the crook of his neck. "My dearest Seanchara, that is one of the many reasons I love you."

A Man of my Word

Diane did not know what time it was when she awoke, she knew she had been dreaming, dreaming of the beautiful, green land that Niri had dreamed of. She saw it clear as day, broad leaves blowing in the breeze. Vines twisting among trees so thick that she could not see between them. The sound of a rushing river nearby, she could smell the water, crisp and clean.

She knew that it would feel like being born again to dive into that water and emerge, naked and dripping. She tried to stretch and cried out from the pain in her arms and ribs. She forced her eyes open when she realized she could not move her arms at all. She was seated on a dirt floor, her back against a post and her arms tied so tight behind her and around the post that she felt for sure her shoulders had been dislocated. Her clothes were wet, and she could not tell if it was blood or urine or something else. Her face felt sticky and swollen, and she was sure something was stabbing her in the ribs on her left side.

When her eyes finally focused enough to see, she saw the carnage everywhere. She was certain this was the old barn behind the house, although she could not remember how she got there. A foul stench filled her nostrils, it was the smell of backed-up sewage and burning meat. She thought for a moment and remembered the words of Father Stag. *It is done when John*

Wilcothe's body has pulled itself apart, he will need to be burned. Reverend Wilcothe, you and your wife will oversee that process, alone. Was that the smell of John Wilcothe's body burning?

As her vision began to focus, she saw the twins directly in front of her. She could not tell who was who, now. Their clothes were torn and filthy. They had been tied to two posts, each girl kneeling, their arms behind their back and secured around the post. A thick rope was tied around each of their waists, binding them to the post behind them. The worst part that Diane could see were the gags. A length of rope, thicker than Diane's wrist was wrapped around the post and pulled tight into the girls' mouths. Its size being larger than their jaws could accommodate, Diane could see the painful stretching of their mouths, and the blood dried on their cheeks where their skin had ripped around the size of the rope.

Diane was watching them closely, looking for signs of breathing. "Desma, Althea, are you awake." She would not ask if they were ok, she knew better.

The twin on the right opened her eyes and began to make choking anguished noises behind the gag. Almost immediately Diane felt the rush of adrenaline and the bloom of pain and anger in her chest.

Lying next to them on the floor was Jackie, her brown hair matted and wet with blood, now drying black. A drying pool of blood stained the dirt floor of the barn around Jackie's head. Diane whispered, "Jackie, Jackie, are you ok? Please talk to me girl, come on, say something."

Jackie did not move, and the twin shook her head "No," but Diane was not sure if she was saying no, she would be ok, or no, she was not ok. But as painful as her position looked, Diane was not going to ask her to clarify. She heard a whimpering to her left but could not turn to look before she heard another voice.

"Oh, shut up you crying, deceitful little whore, you're lucky I did not beat you worse for what you did to your father, the good Lord knows you deserve it. But everyone has to live until tomorrow at the choosing, especially you. There is no such rule about treating you kindly. Your actions caused the death of your father. Do you think you will get to live happily ever after that?"

Diane lowered her head; she did not need to see to know who that voice belonged to the owner. *Judith you cruel bitch*, she thought as she heard multiple footsteps move past her.

A voice she did not recognize, "Have you decided which two?"

Judith's poisonous voice replied, "I have, I wanted to use the two disrespectful albinos, but they are right. Their father's family are all outlaws, grifters, conmen, and killers. As much as I would love the beautiful irony, I do not want to risk giving them a reason to come out of their hovels and hollers. How did you get her cooperation anyway?"

One of the strangers shuffled closer to the twins and came into view. A short, slender red head. "She came to someone I am acquainted with, a witch whose son I caught a few years ago in New Orleans. I found the miserable tub of lard leaving a known safehouse of a Mercer Witch. I had been trying to get one for a while, trying to get ahead of my own deal, you see. I am tired of giving that monster my daughters. So, I catch him, and hold him until Mama shows up, then we have a nice long talk. Either

I bleed baby boy out on the floor, or she gives me a way to bind and destroy the real monster. But she doesn't tell me how to find him. She knows a summoning; but said you cannot summon him and bind him in the same circles. If the summoning isn't precise, it will fail or worse yet, alert him to the fact that someone wants him, who doesn't know the way. This witch, says, I will do you a better deal. His wife wants out, she is trying to free them from their obligations; and would do about anything for them to be able to just live happily ever after somewhere. So, the witch says she will summon her and give her my info, saying I know how to break the bonds of their creation. Says she hates them both but because of their rules, she cannot do anything about it. She will set us up and give me the binding and destruction spells for both of them. All I have to do for her is to forget we ever met."

The woman walked around the twins nodding with approval, "Wow, Judith, you weren't kidding about not liking these girls. Are you sure you don't want to change your mind; I cannot imagine it is going to go well when they get turned loose. Anyway, she showed up on my doorstep one night. Says the witch sent her to me and she wants to set them free from their creators. That he was not able to break out of his mental chains on his own and the witch had sent her to me. Said they will be together, here, and now for this choosing. So, here we are."

Judith said something so quiet Diane could not hear, then said "Everything is in place, I spent many nights in prayer and while I never condone witchcraft, all my prayers; and my faith tells me this is what God wants, and that is what will happen. Come Neeny, let's rest, and pray together. It will be a very long day. We need to prepare the chapel."

As the footsteps retreated to the front of the barn, Diane risked opening her eyes. She could hear Melinda still quietly weeping, the twin that was awake still looked on the verge of explosion, and Jackie still had not moved an inch. She was terrified, what had they been talking about, were they going to try to hurt Father Stag and Mother Moon? That is what it sounded like, but that did not make any sense. Where were the guys, where was Brad? She needed to know her brother was safe. Why had her parents sent her into this hell and where was that voice that had been in her head earlier? She closed her eyes and concentrated, trying to feel for that voice. Crying out to it for help. *If you can hear me, we are in trouble. We are hurt, and scared. Please help me.* Nothing, just the pain of her bonds, and panic threatening to overwhelm her.

Diane spent the next few hours in and out of consciousness, struggling to fight against exhaustion, pain, and hunger. Several times she had heard Melinda crying but when she spoke to her to try and comfort her, the girl did not respond.

The twins did not move, restrained as they were.

At some point, Diane could not tell how long it had been, a group of men from the church stormed into the barn. They began untying the women. Jackie still had not moved and Diane had worried she might have died, but she had groaned a few times so at least she was still breathing. Two men carried her from the barn, and the rest of the women they lined up and rebound their hands, so they had to walk in a very tight line front to back. Her legs ached and she nearly collapsed. They stumbled through the dark yard toward the front doors of the church. Diane heard a shout, and someone grunt in pain, and looked off toward the house where a line of several men were being led in the same way. When they got closer Diane called out, "Brad, are you ok? Where is Brad? Has anyone seen Brad Whistler?"

No one answered as she was shuffled into the same foyer as the night before. She squinted as she came into the brightly lit entryway and came face to face with Judith, on either side of her were two women one was the red head from last night. In the light of the entryway, she was much older than she appeared in the barn. The other woman, a tall blonde, was much younger than both Judith and the red head.

Judith grabbed Diane by the chin. "You will not speak another blasphemous word in this holy place, or I will cut out your tongue, do you understand me? The Reverend has a soft spot for his little sister, but the Reverend is no longer in charge here, and you will respect my rules, or you will be sent back to your parents in pieces."

Diane glared at her but did not speak, she did not know what had changed or why this woman suddenly thought she had the upper hand in this situation but until she knew where Brad was and that he and her new friends were safe, she was going to be very careful.

Ten minutes until eight pm and the doors to the chapel were opened. All of the pews had been moved out of the room except a few lining the walls. Several people were seated in these pews, and Diane saw many of the folks from the regular congregation of The Red Mountain Pentecost Revival. It seemed like just the outsiders had been segregated. No that wasn't right either. On the right side, all the way up by the pulpit was Brad, he was swaying slightly on his feet and two big men stood on either side of him. On the floor at his feet was a large circle. It looked like it was painted onto the carpet of the chapel floor. Letters and numbers in combinations she had never seen before, decorated the inside of the circle along with a large ceramic filled with flowers. She tried to make eye contact with Brad, but he never raised his head. His hands were bound like hers. Directly opposite Brad was another circle on the floor, almost identical, with words, letters, and numbers in combinations she could not interpret. Another language maybe?

It took her a few more seconds to realize why the symbol on the other side caught her eye, Melinda Wilcothe was standing behind it, her hands were bound, and she was crying. As more and more people filed in Diane watched back and forth between the two circles, trying to process what she was seeing, trying to get her mind wrapped around it, it was right there. She needed to focus. She heard the chapel doors slam shut but did not pay any attention, her eyes darted back and forth until they locked on Judith, who had just moved behind Melinda, she turned back toward Brad, where the red-headed woman had moved next to him.

The voice, from yesterday. *Hang on baby, I am almost there.*

Mom, is that you?

No, but she is with me, we are close, just hang on, we lost you for a while, but we are almost there.

Diane started to put the pieces together of what she was seeing. The circles, Brad, Melinda. The apparent change in attitude from Judith.

That woman's voice played in her mind. *Have you decided which two yet?*

Brad and Melinda, bound near those weird circles.

Have you decided which two yet?

Diane screamed as the realization hit her. "Brad no!"

The voice of The Stag echoed through the chapel "What treachery is this? This will not go unpunished."

The red-haired woman reached up to Brad's face, and faster than Diane could react, a flash of silver then one of the men was holding Brad's now open and bleeding throat over the bowl of flowers. Diane wailed in pain as she heard screaming from the other side, she turned back, and two men were holding Melinda Wilcothe in the same position over the bowl as her lifeblood poured out.

Chaos broke out over the chapel, instantly The Stag appeared in the circle in front of Brad where her brother was bleeding to death in a bowl. The man dropped his body in the circle with Father Stag and backed away as he threw back his antlered head and roared in pain and anger. His body seemed to blur and distort. A new scream joined the cacophony as Mother Moon appeared in the circle where Melinda now lay, lifeless.

She screamed at the ceiling. "No one was supposed to be hurt, you lied. He was not supposed to be hurt."

Father Stag, with great effort turned to face his bride, his face a mask of pain and betrayal. "What did you do? Innocent blood spilled by your hands?" His roar was quickly diminishing as he was pulled down to the floor by some invisible hand.

Mother Moon wailed in pain again, "No, No, they lied, they promised to free us."

Father Stag was bleeding now from the eyes, he coughed, and a great gout of blood poured from his mouth.

The red-haired woman howled with laughter. "No more deals you demon bastard. I will take what's mine and you can rot in hell."

A crash behind her, and Diane spun to see her mother, father, and another woman she had never seen, rush into the room. Diane felt the pressure move ahead of them, like getting hit with a wave at the beach. She fell to her knees, more screaming as one of the members of the church reached for other woman, who tapped her on the head; and spoke a word, and the woman fell at her feet. Diane's eyes widened as the older woman with her mother threw a glass jar of some liquid on the painted edge of the circle and it burst into a ball of flame for just a moment. When the smoke cleared, she watched in horror as Father Stag, kneeling with his great horned head bowed toward the floor, faded from view. Her mother stared for a moment at Brad's body on the ground and ran to him, then shouted at the other woman to release the Mother Moon.

Diane's father ran over to her and began to untie her. "I am so sorry, sweetheart, we have been trying to get here, but there will be time to explain later.

She wrapped her arms around his neck, exhausted but relieved. "Daddy, they killed Brad, you have to help, they killed him."

"I know baby, I know, your mom has him and if anyone can help, she can. Just come with me. Let's get you safe."

A voice boomed through the chapel, shaking the walls. "I told you what would happen if anyone interfered with The Choosing, and I am a man who keeps his promises. Clan Wilcothe will parish this day. Witches, you have done well, and your deed here today will be remembered at the Temple of the Mother, but you will take your consort and let me continue my work."

Diane's mother cried, "Lord Seanchara, please, my son, my daughter."

Father Stag's voice roared again, "Go, you cannot pass through the veil twice. Your heroism will not go unrewarded. But my gratitude is not without limits."

Diane watched in horror as her mother, father, and the other woman with them, began backing out of the blasted chapel doors. Diane noticed several parishioners attempting to leave with them, but they could not seem to cross the threshold.

That woman's voice was in her head. *Be brave Diane, it's almost over. We will be together again soon.*

She looked back at Mother Moon who was spinning circles, looking very much like a caged animal trying to escape death. She saw Judith backing toward the baptismal tank at the back of the stage.

Out of the space in front of her, a shape formed, large and apelike, covered in coarse, black fur. A long arm reached out and caught the blonde woman that had been with Judith by the hair, as she ran for the door.

"Oathbreaker." It hissed through a mouth filled with pointed teeth and ringed with feelers or tentacles. It yanked her hair back, and the red-haired woman screamed in protest. "Shut up Neeny, you just gave me another daughter, and you don't even get more time for this one."

He leaned forward and screamed into the woman's face. "Look at your mother, your precious Neeny, she did this to you, she sacrificed your sister, Dorthea, and now she has given me you as well. I wonder if she will move on to your daughters next. Before the woman could reply, he rammed his other hand down her throat muffling her scream, a spray of blood from her ripped cheeks as his muscular arm forced his way into her mouth. Her jaw distended, her teeth dislodging. He had his arm, almost to the elbow, down her throat when he began to shake her back and forth violently. Diane realized he was pulling her guts loose and began to wretch. She could hear screaming and people running. But the sound of Father Stag, if this monster was still him, killing, drowned out everything else.

She tried not to look but found every time she heard someone else screaming, she was compelled to. She heard a wet thumping sound and looked back to see the monster with Althea in one hand and Desma in the other. He was pounding their bodies together. Using one twin to beat the other to death. She screamed again and he dropped the twins and jumped into the next crowd, stepping on Jackie's head, and crushing her skull underneath a hideously clawed foot when he landed.

Diane could hear Mother Moon screaming. "No, love. Please no more. This is my fault, I just wanted us free. I didn't know, I was blinded by my love for you and did not see their deception. Please kill me, leave the rest of this family."

He jumped from one side of the chapel to stand just outside the circle where she was trapped. He pulled her out of the circle, she struggled to get away, but it was clear even she was no match for him. He pushed her head down and screamed, blood and spit flying from his grotesque mouth. "Look at her, look at what your betrayal did, you killed her. You did that. How could you?"

Mother Moon stared only at the ground between them. "I am sorry my love, I only wanted us to have the choice, for our lives to be our own, I just wanted you for myself, even if only for a little while."

"Your selfishness and ignorance has cost the lives of this entre clan Valkyrie."

She flinched at the statement as if struck.

"You were blind, well now you will be blind forever more. Let her lifeless body be the last image on your eyes."

He spun her around and pulled her close to his body, the tentacles on his face slithered across her cheeks and began to dig their way into her eye sockets. Mother Moon screamed and thrashed in his arms as he pulled the eyes from their sockets and one by one, the tentacles slid them into his mouth, and he swallowed.

He tossed her aside and leaped across the floor to the red-headed woman "Neeny, you will not die, not yet. We have years left before you owe me your life, or yet another daughter. I suggest you run like hell and do not ever look back. I will see you in a few years." At this, he jumped into the last remaining crowd at the back corner. It took him only moments to tear them apart.

He walked back toward Diane. They were, as far as she could tell, the only living things in the chapel. Mother Moon had vanished, that red-haired woman, and Judith were both gone. He carried an arm, as casually as one might carry their lunch. Diane tried to backpedal, to find an escape route away from what was coming next. The monster reached out and caught her by the collar. "Please, please sir, I don't want to die, I want to go home. Please let me go home."

"I am so sorry child, I am sorry that this is your introduction to Mercer, I am sorry for the loss of your brother, and your friends. I promise you, one day soon, you are going to wake up to the most amazing life you can imagine. But for now."

He released her collar and brushed a single finger down her cheek, and Diane Whistler fell dead at his feet.

The sun was rising outside The Red Mountain Pentecost Revival, the first rays of daylight were shining through the block glass windows of the chapel.

In the middle of the chapel floor, in a puddle of blood and gore of his own making, Lord Seanchara, The Stag of Red Mountain, was weeping. He had taken a form as close to human as he got. His bare torso heaved as he sobbed. A slim black hand cautiously reached out to lay on his great shoulder.

"Is your rage sated old friend?"

He did not look up, but he gently brushed his hand across the delicate one on his shoulder. "I did what I promised I would do, nothing more, nothing less."

"Look in my eyes Guardian and you will find no judgment. Only sympathy and concern."

"Thank you, Niri." He said as he rose and turned to look her in the eyes.

"How did you know?"

"She came straight to me of course. Told me of her folly and the repercussions. Her betrayal of your trust and ours. She offered to exile herself, I told her the Elders would speak on it, as is our way. But just as I cannot imagine our world without Lord Seanchara in it, I cannot imagine it without Elder Valkyrie either. But that is a dilemma for another day. She knows the witch responsible for giving the women their information on how to trap and hurt you. That will have to be dealt with. It would be my honor if you let us deal with her. Did you kill the real monsters responsible for this?"

"The Reverend's wife somehow escaped through a broom closet with no exit or windows and has moved beyond my sight. So that will need to be figured out at some point. The Reverend himself seems to have been burned with his brother."

"If you will forgive me Lord Seanchara, I will not presume to understand either one of you. But I do know a bit about love and duty. Only you know if forgiveness lives in your heart. But I know that only pain and regret live in hers. Can I assist you in getting everyone back home? Would you like to show me who was chosen?"

"Butchered by The Harvester and escorted to the Chambers of the Veil by Mother Mercer herself. These four will have quite a story to tell when they awaken."

Mysterious Ways

Judith knelt in her small chamber under The Red Mountain Pentecost Revival. The room had nothing but a small basin, a stand for her bible, a lantern, and a cot. She had been coming down here for years seeking the Lord's face in prayer. If she was honest, she had also spent a good deal of time down here, hiding from Reverend Wilcothe. He was a boorish man, and a pervert. She had been relieved when it was revealed to her in prayer that she was to kill the Reverend and burn his body along with his rapist brother.

She bowed her head and prayed. "Heavenly Father, please forgive your servant. I have failed in my great work, and I seek your guidance. The demons and witches still live. Please Lord, if it is your will that I smite your enemies and rid the earth of their filth. Grant me the strength. Allow me to lead your host of angels as they meet your enemies in battle. In your most holy name, Amen."

Before she even opened her eyes Judith could immediately feel she was not alone in the small room. Nothing could have slipped past her; she was facing the only entrance. But she heard the breathing just behind her left ear. She spun and was face to face with the largest German Shepard she had ever seen. She felt no fear. Nothing could be in this space that was not ordained by God himself and if this animal meant her harm, then it was

God's will, and there was nothing she could do about it. The dog leaned its body against her and began nuzzling at her hand. Sniffing at the stains of the blood of Melinda Wilcothe. Then it leaned in close to her face, opened it's great mouth, and began to whisper. As it did, a plan began to form in her mind. As clear a picture as she had ever seen. She would lead a host of angels against the enemies of righteousness. It might not take the shape she had originally thought, but her faith in her mission and her role in God's great plan was renewed.

Judith smiled broadly as she stroked the dog's fur.

The Chambers of the Veil

"Come back now child, that's it, follow my voice. I know it is peaceful there, but you have rested long enough. Your family needs you."

Niri Agash, Mother Mercer, stood in a small stone chamber; the room was lit by a single candle in a wall sconce. She remembered the day this chamber was completed; its walls were engraved with intricate carvings. Scenes from the beginning of Mercer, from her exodus from the farm, her young children and Binlai in tow. Somewhere, on these many stones, there is an exact replica of the summoning ritual her mother had given her during her first dream of Mercer.

It was hard for her to believe they were all gone now. All four daughters, Binlai, and so many others. But here she remained, seemingly removed from the flow of time. Of all of Mercer, none of the first generation of women who had come to her in those early days still lived. A couple of the Elders were granddaughters of the original Mercer women. But times had been hard on them in those early days. Many memories, like these walls, had worn smooth with time. Funny how events that had such depth and power at the time could become so two dimensional.

Her first meeting with Seanchara, the flood, awakening in the arms of the father after passing through the veil. All of it; dimmed now, with the passage of time. Decades ago, she had spent a day fishing on the banks of a great river with Seanchara and Valkyrie. She asked them if memory faded for them as it did for her. Seanchara's response broke her heart.

Mother, I remember every face, every loss, every death. Every single person I have sent through the veil, either gently or brutally, the look of terror in their dying eyes is etched upon my mind for all eternity.

It is no wonder Valkyrie had tried to free him. What a burden, Niri knew his heart, perhaps not as well as Valkyrie, but she knew him for the poet and artist he was. His tenderness, his love of children, and of all life in general. As terrifying as he could be, and one was right to be fearful of him, she could not imagine the weight of that burden.

Lost in her nostalgia as she was, it took her longer than it should have to realize the young woman on the stone slab in the middle of the room had not stirred when called.

Niri stepped closer and laid her hand on the woman's forehead, the skin was still ice cold.

Stubborn, Niri thought, *which may serve her well one day, far from here, but for now, this child needed to get to work.*

She placed her other hand on the woman's still, cold, chest. "Diane Whistler, that's enough, it is time for you to come back. Push through the veil child, we have much to discuss, and your mother, father and aunt are all waiting for you."

Diane's eyes snapped open, shock and horror on her face as she drew in her first breath in more than a year.

Niri smiled down at her, "There you are child, breath for me, it will only take a moment to get things going automatically again. You are through the worst of it. That's it Diane. I know it is confusing now but soon you will know all there is to know. Besides, if I don't get you up and out of here soon, I fear those Lewis girls are going to kick the door down looking for you."

Diane's voice was scratchy and hoarse from long lack of use. "Althea?"

Niri smiled at her. "Funnily enough baby, your name was the first thing she said when we woke her up. I think Desma gave her the silent treatment for fifteen whole minutes over that little oversight."

Niri knew that this young lady would have a lot of catching up to do, being dead for a year or so left one with some gaps, but if Seanchara was right, and he usually was, she would catch up, and when she did, there were great things coming her way.

The End.

About the Author

Punk rock bastard son of country folk healers and big tent evangelicals. Neo-Pagan and keeper of the Aging Elvinian Psycho Sexual Vaudvillian Vibration. D.O. lives in the midwest where he experiments with taming wild animals with string band instrumentation; and roasting meats between writing novels.

Read more at doscissom.com.